Flaky's Big Dream

Dan Zobrist

Illustrated By Marylou Blakeslee

To Sasquatch Books

Dan Zobrist

Lonely Kayak Publishing
PO Box 1168
Sequim, WA 98382

10 9 8 7 6 5 4 3 2 1
Printed in the United States of America

Library of Congress Control Number: 2017952996
ISBN: 978-1-944887-24-7

Cover Image: Marylou Blakeslee, Topeka Glacier
Illustrator: Marylou Blakeslee
Cover Design: Marcia Breece, Publishing Partners
Interior Design: Marcia Breece, Publishing Partners

The power of imagination makes us infinite.

– John Muir

This book is dedicated to all the people who love the wild places in the world and especially to those rangers and others who protect them. I especially want to thank Steve Schaller at Glacier Bay National Park, who taught me how to write a children's program.

Once upon a time, there was a
snowflake named Flaky
who lived high in the mountains of Alaska,
the highest coastal mountains in the world.
Flaky was a happy little snowflake
with a big dream.

He wanted to move mountains.

Some of the other residents of these high mountains thought that Flaky's dream was silly. "Imagine," they all agreed, "a snowflake who wants to move mountains."

The bald eagle soaring high in the winds thought it was funny.

The mountain goat standing on his tiny, narrow ledge chuckled at such a wild dream.

The moose laughed, wiggled her ears and slurped up tasty water plants.

There was even a humpback whale swimming in a deep fjord who heard the news that a snowflake wanted to move a mountain and he laughed and laughed from his big belly.

4

Flaky's feelings were hurt a little bit but he didn't care.
He had his own dream.
Do you sometimes have big dreams of things you want to do?
Are you afraid to tell someone because they might laugh?

Flaky had only one problem. He didn't know how to move mountains. So he asked his best friend, Glacey, who would never make fun of him. You see, Glacey was a glacier and he moved mountains all the time.

Glacey was a long river of solid ice. He started up high in the mountain range where it snowed all the time, and he traveled all the way downhill to the ocean. Because Glacey ended up at the ocean, he was a tidewater glacier.

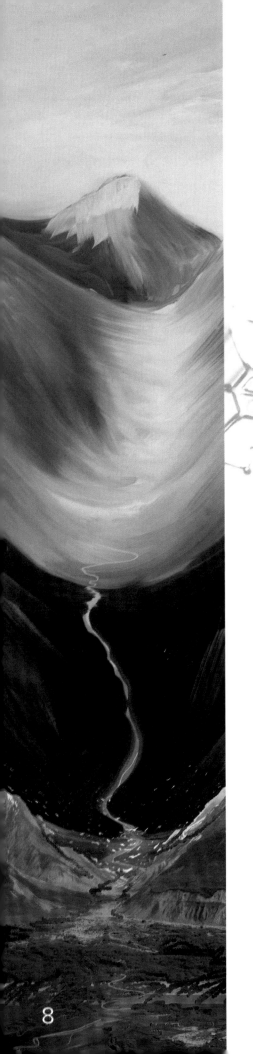

And like any other river, Glacey moved. Have you seen how a little stream can travel downhill and curve around bends and over rocks? Little streams can pick up rocks and sand in one place and carry them to another place and just drop them.

Glaciers can do the same thing. But because a glacier is made up of solid ice, it is very heavy, and it can push the rocks and sand in front of it. In fact, it is so powerful that it can make sand out of the rocks by crushing them.

And that's how a tidewater glacier moves mountains. It grinds up the mountain into small pieces and then carries the pieces to the ocean, where they get carried away by the salt water to somewhere else.

Flaky loved to watch Glacey pluck rocks from the mountains, grind them into sand and drop them off many miles away into the ocean. How cool is that? Flaky wanted to do the same thing.

So, one day Flaky asked his friend, "Will you tell me how you move mountains?"

Glacey was surprised at the question. "You live in the mountains, Flaky. Why do you want to move them?"

Flaky thought hard about that question because he liked Glacey very much and wanted to give him a good answer. "I like my high mountains because I can see everything that is going on down below. But the most beautiful things to see are the valleys that have a long U-shape to their sides. Those are the ones that you make and I want to move a mountain to make one of those U-shaped valleys.

"Yes," said Glacey. "When I move mountains around I like to smooth out the sides of the steep valleys that the rivers make. Ok, I'll share with my best friend how you move a mountain.

"First thing to remember is that you don't move a mountain all at once. That would be too hard to do. You move a mountain just a little bit at a time. When I slide downhill like a river, I take a little bit of the mountain with me. I do this with a trick I know. When I press my ice against the sides of the mountain, I melt a little bit and then quickly refreeze, so that rocks get stuck in my ice. Then I use those rocks to scrape against the mountain until it rubs off into little rocks and sand.

"Before you know it, I am on my way to moving a whole bunch of the mountain all the way downhill into the ocean. It's fun."

Flaky listened closely to each word that his friend shared.
He couldn't wait to try it himself. He couldn't believe that his big dream would come true.
Early the next morning Flaky flexed up all his strength and pressed as hard as he could against the mountain.
But nothing happened.
He didn't melt. He didn't refreeze with a bunch of rocks stuck in his ice. He didn't move a mountain.
He tried again. But it was no use. He just wasn't strong enough to move a mountain.
Flaky was very sad.

Glacey saw that his best friend was not happy.
"Why the sad face, Flaky?"

"I am discouraged," said Flaky. "I can't even move a grain of sand, let alone a mountain. Maybe I'll just quit trying."

"You don't reach your dream by quitting," his friend advised. "You just need some help. You live on the highest coastal mountain range in the world. It is so high that it reaches clouds that are full of snowflakes. You need to ask all the snowflakes in the sky to come down from the clouds and help you move this mountain."

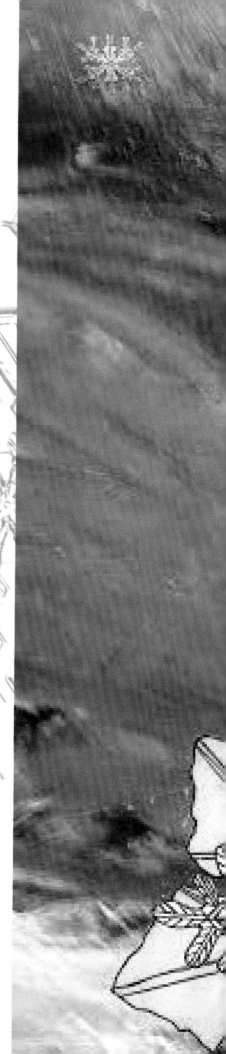

Flaky looked up and saw that Glacey was right. Up above he saw clouds that were full of snowflakes. With the loudest voice he could, he called all the snowflakes to join him in his wonderful dream—to move a mountain. And then a zillion snowflakes began falling from the sky. Fat flakes and skinny flakes and funny flakes and flakes that sparkled with all the colors of the rainbow joined Flaky on top of the mountain.

Glacey watched all this happen and he was proud of his friend for not quitting. "That's the way to do it, Flaky. Good start. Now tell the snowflakes to pack real tight together, as tight as they can."

$\mathcal{A}$s the snowflakes got tighter and tighter,
Flaky, on the bottom, began to get rounder and rounder under all
the weight until the other flakes started sliding around on him.
They couldn't stay put.
And then it happened: the weight of all the little snowflakes
became so heavy that they started sliding down the mountain.

$\mathcal{F}$laky watched himself turn blue. He loved it.
He was blue just like his friend Glacey.
Glaciers are blue because they are packed really tight. That lets
them absorb all the light rays of the sun except the blue ones. The
blue light rays are then bounced back for everybody to see.

"Wheee," said Flaky. He was sliding down the mountain with all his snowflake friends. He remembered what Glacey taught him and used the little rocks he picked up along the way to scrape the side of the mountain into sand.

"Success," cried Flaky, "I'm a river of ice and I'm moving this big old mountain all the way to the ocean, one grain of sand at a time. Look at me Glacey! Look at me go."

"Great job, Flaky. You're making a beautiful U-shaped valley under your glacier ice. But if you want to see it, then you have to retreat. Just start melting your ice at the front and you'll go back up the mountain where you were before."

Flaky was having too much fun to retreat. He wanted to keep advancing even after he got to the tidewater. He wanted to go all the way to the Pacific Ocean. But he knew he would need help.

"Will you join me?" he asked Glacey. "Together
we can really move this mountain and
carve out a beautiful valley."

Glacey thought about his friend's offer.
He had been building up a lot of snow
at his source on the mountaintop.
When a glacier has lots of snow
up high in the mountains
then it can slide downhill.

"Why not?" laughed Glacey. "It's been a long time
since I advanced, so maybe I'll join you.
Together we can really move these mountains."

And so they did.

Glacey and Flaky joined together and
began carving out a beautiful U-shaped valley
that would someday become a national park for all to
enjoy. Other glaciers nearby saw what they were doing
and asked if they could join in the fun.

"Of course," shouted Flaky and Glacey with a laugh, as
the two friends scraped and plucked their way
through the mountains.

Then all the animals that didn't believe in Flaky's dream
saw the beautiful world that Flaky was creating and they
became very happy.

"Hooray for Flaky," they cheered.

And onward they marched. Some glaciers traveled a hundred miles from their source and all joined together into one glacier to be a mighty carver of the mountains. The glaciers plowed through forests and pushed into the ocean until they met the famous naturalist, John Muir, who was sitting at his campsite watching them.

26

John Muir was a lover of mountains and glaciers and was so impressed that he gave the glacier a new name. "I've watched you travel all the way from the top of the mountains to the Pacific Ocean. That is a grand adventure if I've ever seen one. From this day forward, you will forever be known as 'The Grand Pacific Glacier.'"

Interactive Study Guide

1. What was Flaky's big dream?

2. What is a tidewater glacier?

3. How is a glacier like a river?

4. How can you tell that a valley was made by a glacier?

5. How does a tidewater glacier move a mountain?

6. Why did Flaky need help to reach his dream?

7. Why are glaciers blue?

❄ ❄ ❄ ❄ ❄ ❄ ❄ ❄ ❄ ❄ ❄ ❄ ❄ ❄ ❄

Additional Resources

—Collier, Michael. Sculpted by Ice: Glaciers and the Alaska Landscape, Anchorage, Alaska, Alaska Natural History Association, 2004.

—Wiley, Sally D. Blue Ice in Motion: The Story of Alaska's Glaciers,   Anchorage, Alaska, Alaska Natural History Association, 1990.

—Ferguson, Sue A. Glaciers of North America: A Field Guide, Fulcrum Publishing, 1992.

—Hocker, Katherine, Frozen in Motion, Anchorage, Alaska, Alaska Natural History Association, 2006.

—Muir, John Stikeen by John Muir Nevada City, Ca., Dawn Pubns 1998

—Wilson, Barbara, Icebergs and Glaciers: Life at the Frozen Edge, San Luis Obispo, Ca. Blake Publishing, 1990.